UP on Bob

Words and pictures by
Mary Sullivan

HOUGHTON MIFFLIN HARCOURT
Boston   New York

To Joseph, Dianne, Michael, and Patrick

hmhco.com

The illustrations in this book were digitally drawn and colored.
The text type was set in Adobe Caslon Pro.
The display type was hand lettered.

Library of Congress Cataloging-in-Publication Data is on file.

ISBN: 978-1-328-99471-4

Manufactured in China
SCP 10 9 8 7 6 5 4 3 2 1
4500781726

This is Bob.

Up on
the bed
Bob has work
to do.

The work is hard.

But Bob does not mind.

Bob likes hard work.

Hard work pays off.

There.

Now everything
is perfect.

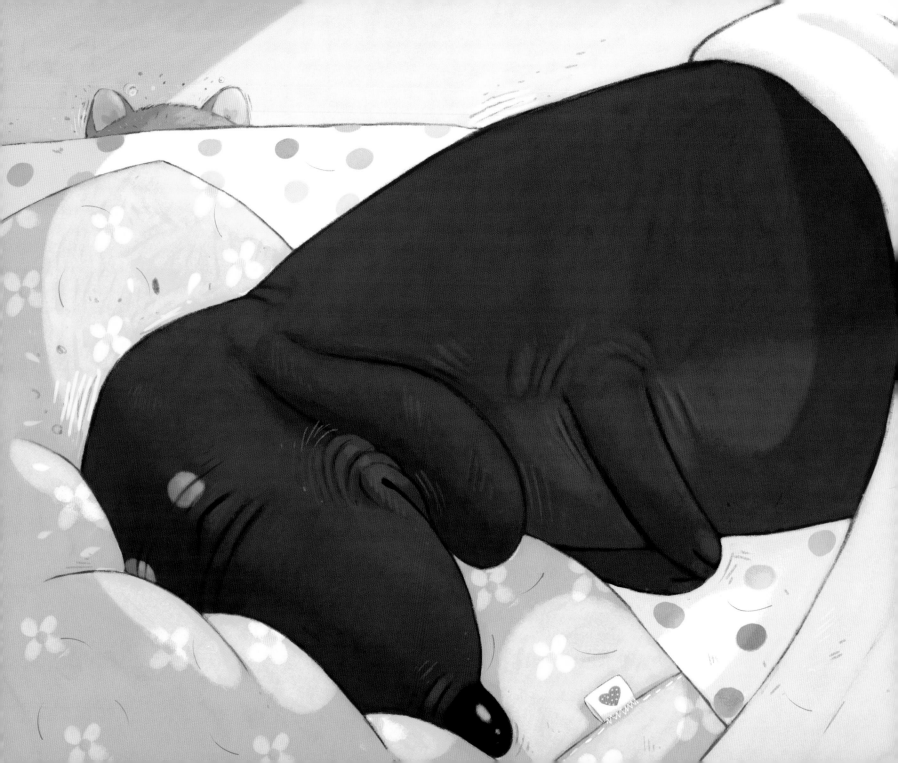

Now Bob can sleep all day.

Uh-oh.

Suddenly everything
is not perfect.

Someone is watching Bob.

Bob cannot sleep if Someone is watching.

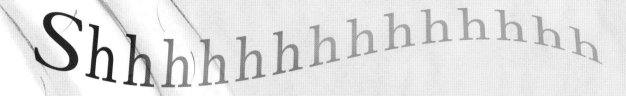

Shhhhhhhhhhhhh

Lay still, Bob.

Pretend you are
sleeping.

Maybe Someone
will go away.

Is Someone leaving?

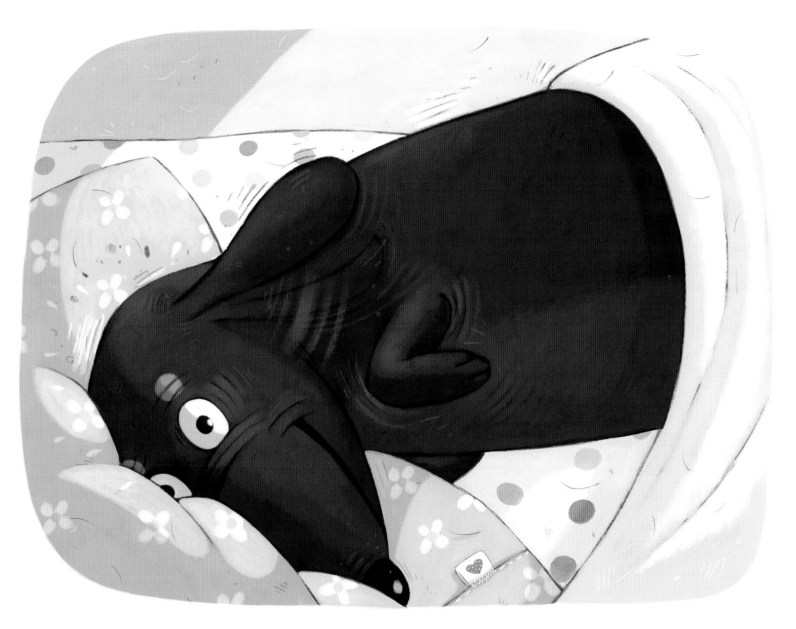

Is Someone gone?

Up on Bob . . .

Someone has
work to do.

The work is hard.

But Someone does not mind.

Someone likes hard work.

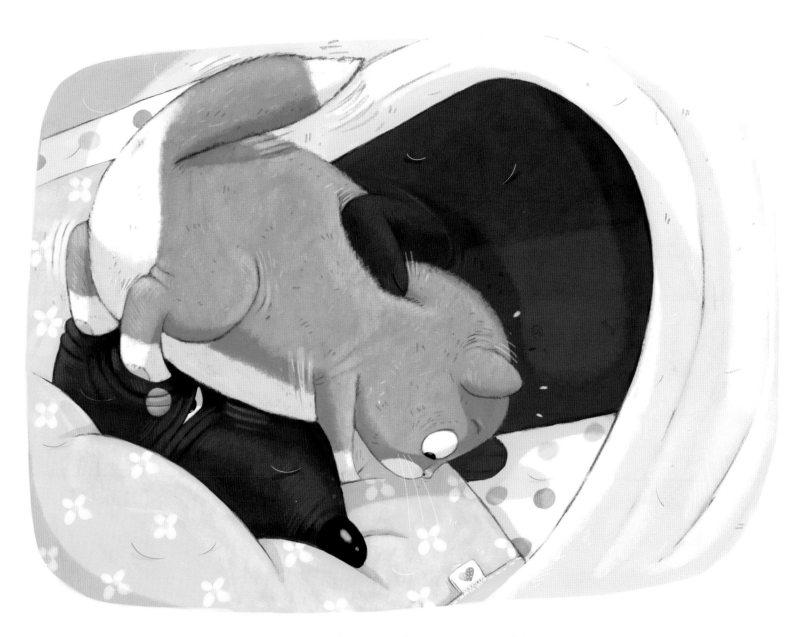

Hard work pays off.

There.

Now everything
is perfect.

Now Bob can sleep all day.